PHANTOM HEARTS

ROSIE TALBOT   SARAH MAXWELL

SCHOLASTIC

Published in the UK by Scholastic, 2024
1 London Bridge, London, SE1 9BG
Scholastic Ireland, 89E Lagan Road, Dublin Industrial Estate, Glasnevin, Dublin, D11 HP5F

SCHOLASTIC and associated logos are trademarks and/or
registered trademarks of Scholastic Inc.

Text © Rosie Talbot, 2024
Illustrations © Sarah Maxwell, 2024
Cover illustration by Sarah Maxwell

The right of Rosie Talbot and Sarah Maxwell to be identified
as the author and illustrator of this work has been asserted by them
under the Copyright, Designs and Patents Act 1988.

ISBN 978 07023 3340 8

A CIP catalogue record for this book is available from the British Library.

Printed and bound in Great Britain by Clays Ltd, Elcograf S.p.A.
Paper made from wood grown in sustainable forests and other controlled sources.

1 3 5 7 9 10 8 6 4 2

www.scholastic.co.uk

FOR THE GIRL I WAS, I'M SORRY I WASN'T STRONGER.
R. T.

TO MY FAMILY AND FRIENDS, WHO CHEERED ME ON WHILE MAKING THIS. TO MY BEST FRIEND AND WIFE, JUDY, WHO I COULDN'T HAVE DONE THIS WITHOUT THE LOVE AND SUPPORT OF. AND TO THE QUEER COMMUNITY, WHOSE LOVE SHOULD BE REPRESENTED AND CELEBRATED - ALWAYS.
S. M.

CHAPTER ONE

CLICK

CLICK

HUH?

OH, SORRY, JUST THINKING.

EARTH TO MAL!

WE LOST YOU THERE FOR A SEC.

TOO ANXIOUS TO WORK.

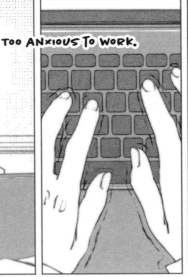

UGH

ACCOUNT
327.40

TODAY
THE LILYPAD

PHOTO CONTEST
APPLICATION FORM

FEE: £300

NAME: _____ ABOUT _____

IT'S MY FUNERAL.

EMIL
100 3,833 1,516
POSTS FOLLOWERS FOLLOWING

EMIL
CREATING, QUESTING, RESTING
DISABLED
FOLLOW MESSAGE

MESSAGES

BONNIE:
ent a photo

BONNIE:
Finn's here so Russ probably won't show. Just as well you don't like him anymore. You on your way?

MALIA:
Coursework. Remember?

BONNIE:
Didn't you sort that? Trust me, it's worth the money.

TYPE

...

TYPE

MALIA:
Fifteen minutes

I CAN'T BELIEVE HE'S JUST GONE. THEY'RE ALL GONE.

... IN THE SUMMER OF '95 THE KILLER GOES QUIET, LEAVING THE TOWN STIFLED BY GRIEF,

AND THE VICTIM'S FAMILIES FACING THEIR WORST NIGHTMARE –

THE POSSIBILITY THEY WILL NEVER KNOW WHAT HAPPENED TO THEIR LOVED ONES.

SILENCE IS NEVER QUIET.

IT'S THE HIGH RING INSIDE YOUR BRAIN THAT SUMMONS ALL THE LITTLE MIND GOBLINS TO WHISPER THE WORST PARTS OF YOU BACK TO YOURSELF.

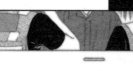

CHAPTER THREE

MARTIN BACOTE ⋯

COMMENTS

♥ LIKED BY AUTHOR
THE DRIVER WAS 100% DRUNK

♥ LIKED BY AUTHOR
WHAT A HORRIBLE THING TO DO TO A BUNCH OF POOR TEENAGERS.

♥ LIKED BY AUTHOR
SCUMBAG

BZZZ

♥ ♡ ◁

● ○ ○ ○ •

LIKED BY 3400 OTHERS

VIEW ALL COMMENTS

ADD A COMMENT...

ELLA:

Did you see the cinema trip on the group chat? Do you think you'll make it? I promise we'll see a happy movie.

BONNIE:

...

JAMES:

...

BONNIE:

Are you coming to school today?

LIFT

HOSTS
A Handbook of the Afterlife

It is generally accepted that the majority of spirits linger due to unfinished business. This could be positive, such as connecting with a lost loved one to deliver a final message, or potentially harmful, like exacting revenge. People who died before their time in tragic or sudden circumstances are more likely to linger.

Everyone has the potential to see ghosts but their ability to do so is usually directly connected to the ghost themselves. The stronger the spirit, the more people they can appear to. Often, they appear to people they believe can help them pass on or people who are somehow connected to their death, even generations later.

Soul groups – a common phenomenon when ghosts travel in groups, connected because they share either a location or time of death. They are most commonly found at sites of larger-scale disasters. Helping such ghosts is a challenge because they must move on as a group, and each soul must solve their unfinished business before they can do so. Luckily, in such cases their unfinished business is usually their collective cause of death.

UNFINISHED BUSINESS. THAT MAKES SENSE.

BENNY, THE GHOST I SAW, HUNG AROUND TO EXPOSE MY MUM'S MANAGER FOR FRAUD. WHEN MUM FIRED HER, BENNY MOVED ON.

IF YOU'RE SEEING SOME OF THE KIDS WHO DIED, THEN THEY'RE RESTLESS SOULS UNABLE TO MOVE ON UNTIL THEY RESOLVE WHATEVER ISSUE IS KEEPING THEM EARTHBOUND. PROBABLY THEY NEED TO UNDERSTAND WHY THEY DIED.

IFRA PEARL DELAYS TOUR DUE TO PERSONAL TRAGEDY

CHAPTER · FOUR

CLICK

I HATE SHOWERS.

IT'S THE PLACE MY BRAIN IS THE SHITTIEST TO ME.

IN THE QUIET, ALONE UNDER THE WATER, MY NEGATIVE THOUGHTS BECOME A FLOOD.

I WISH I HAD A BRAIN THAT WAS NICE TO ME.

I CAN'T.

I'LL JUST MAKE EVERYTHING WORSE.

I spend every day hating you, thinking that if I can just make it true,
Things will be simple again. Because seeing you this other way,
Wrapped in fast-paced fury, just wrecks my day.
We can't run from this, so maybe I'll settle and accept who I am,
While you test my mettle. Battle weary, because you'd rather fight.
Set on self-destruct, I'm waiting for us. If we can just get through because
I can't sit back and let this happen to you

CLICK
CLICK

PRESS

I GOT THEM SO WRONG.

MALIA?

COMMENTS

LIKED BY AUTHOR
THE DRIVER WAS 100% DRUNK

LIKED BY AUTHOR
WHAT A HORRIBLE THING TO
DO TO A BUNCH OF POOR
TEENAGERS.

LIKED BY AUTHOR
SCUMBAG

BE CAREFUL.

SOMETIMES THE TRUTH IS THE HARDEST THING TO HEAR.

BUT YOU'RE AS STONE-HEARTED AS THEY COME.

CHAPTER SIX

CHAPTER SEVEN

JAMIE'S AMAZING AT MAKE-UP, ELLA IS SO ON IT WITH HER HORSE RIDING, YOU HAVE YOUR PHOTOGRAPHY AND YOU'RE SO *TALENTED.*

I'VE TRIED, REALLY TRIED TO FIND SOMETHING I'M AMAZING AT.

SHE'S JEALOUS OF ME?

JUST ONCE, I WANTED TO BE THE BEST AT SOMETHING—

I'M NOT SAYING YOU DO THIS, BUT WITH JAMIE AND ELLA, IT'S ALWAYS A COMPETITION, YOU KNOW?

SHE DIDN'T KNOW EMIL'S SECRET WAS OUT AND AT RISK OF EXPOSING HER LIST OF CLIENTS.

YEAH, I KNOW.

LOOK, YOU CAN RELAX ABOUT THE CHEATING THING. THE SCHOOL AREN'T GOING TO FIND OUT IT WAS YOU.

IT'S NOT BONNIE.

SHE DIDN'T DO THIS.

HOW CAN YOU BE SURE? I KNOW EMIL WAS CAREFUL, BUT—

SHE DIDN'T KNOW I TOLD HER ABOUT THE INVESTIGATION.

TRUST ME, OK? YOUR SECRET'S SAFE.

CHUG CHUG

RUSTLE

RUSTLE

CHAPTER EIGHT

CHATTER

CHATTER

CHATTER

THAT.

JOURNALIST?

I ACTUALLY MEANT BECAUSE OF THE JOURNALIST.

THE ONE THREATENING MALIA.

HE'S GOING TO PUBLISH A NASTY ARTICLE ABOUT MY DAD UNLESS I GIVE HIM AN INSIDE SCOOP.

BUT WE ONLY HAVE TWO DAYS TO FIND WHO DID THIS.

MAYBE I SHOULD LET HIM INTERVIEW ME... TRY AND DELAY THE ARTICLE.

BAD IDEA.

HE'LL JUST MANIPULATE YOU AND SPIN WHATEVER YOU SAY TO FIT HIS NARRATIVE.

I'VE SEEN THE PRESS DO IT A THOUSAND TIMES WITH IFRA. NEVER TALK TO THE MEDIA UNLESS YOU'RE THE ONE IN CONTROL.

THEN WE PROVE IT WAS FINN.

CHAPTER NINE

I FAILED.

THE WHOLE WORLD WILL HATE HIM.

WHEN HE WAKES UP ...

... WILL HE EVEN WANT TO LIVE?

MUTTER

MUTTER

WHERE ARE YOU GOING?

BUS DRIVER D

RIGH

TIME TO TAKE CONTROL
OF THE STORY.

SOME LOVES SNEAK UP ON YOU ...

... BUT OTHER TIMES ...

... IT HITS YOU LIKE LIGHTNING.

TAP

TAP

TAP

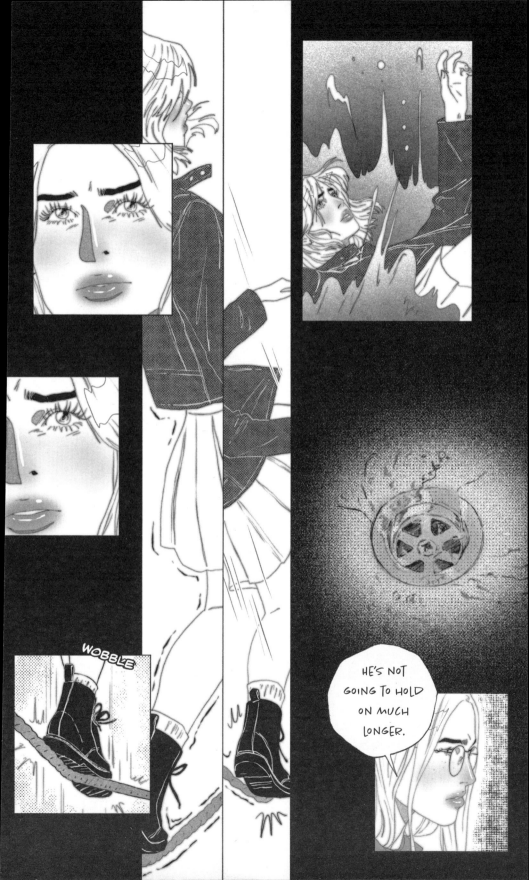

CHAPTER TEN

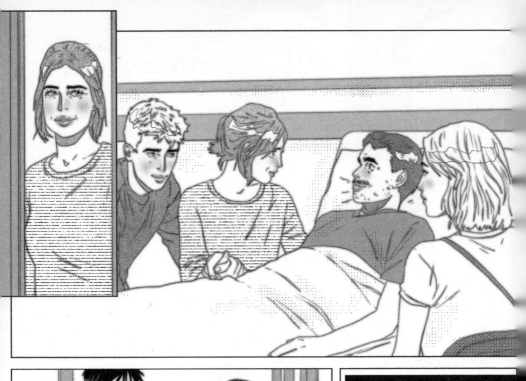

SNIFF

SNIFF

CHAPTER ELEVEN

PHOTO CONTEST
APPLICATION FORM

AME: _____

TELL US ABOUT YOUR SUBMISSION:

SOMETIMES, WE ONLY GET PEOPLE FOR A HEARTBEAT, THAT'S IT.

IT DOESN'T MAKE THEM LESS IMPORTANT...

BLUSH

DO YOU KNOW HOW TO PLAY UNO?

WE ALL CARRY PHANTOM HEARTS THROUGH LIFE WITH US.

MAYBE THEY'RE GIFTED FROM SOMEONE WE'VE KNOWN ALL OUR LIVES,

OR MAYBE FROM THOSE WE KNEW FOR ONLY THE BRIEFEST MOMENT, THE BRIEFEST HEARTBEAT.

THEY ALL MATTER.

I MATTER.